HELP! HOUSEHOLD EMERGENCY & LIFELINE PHONE NUMBERS

EMERGENCY

POLICE STATION	
FIRE STATION	
AMBULANCE	
GAS	
ELECTRICITY	
WATER	
CLOSEST EMERGENCY ROOM	
LOST PET	

MEDICAL

FAMILY DOCTOR			
PEDIATRICIAN			
DENTIST			
PET EMERGENCY			
DRUGSTORE (24-HOUR)			
ANIMAL/ INSECT BITES			
RAPE HOTLINE		DRUG HOTLINE	
SUICIDE HOTLINE		POISON HOTLINE	

FAMILY, FRIENDS & NEIGHBORS

Name	Address	Home Phone	Office Phone

IN CASE OF ACCIDENT OR INJURY NOTIFY:

Name	Address	Home Phone	Office Phone

The Sweet Nellie HomeFile

THE ESSENTIAL HOUSEHOLD ORGANIZER AND DIRECTORY

Pat Ross

WATERCOLORS BY KATE WILLIAMS

VIKING STUDIO BOOKS

Contents

I. HOUSEHOLD AND FAMILY RECORDS   7

Household & Family Records

Family Tree

Allergies

Name	Allergy	Reaction	Treatment/Medication

Name	Blood Type	Notes
Nancy	O Negative	

Record of Hospitalization

Name	Date	Reason	Doctor	Hospital
Nancy	March 20, 1987	Hysterectomy	Ronald Peterson	GBMC

Childhood Illness / Disease Record

Name	Illness	Treatment	Date	Doctor

Immunization Record

Name	Immunization	Date	Doctor
Nancy	Tetanus	Dec. 1996	Dr. Ramsey

Name	Dentist	Notes

Family Medications

Name	Brand	Generic	Pharmacy	Prescription Number	Quantity/Size/Dosage

Financial

Bank Accounts

Bank	User Name(s)	Account Type & Number	ATM Card Number	Information Number

Credit Cards

Card Name	User Name(s)	Number	Expiration Date	Lost/Stolen Hotline

Investments

Type	Broker/Bank	Investor	Notes

Taxes

Accountant	Forms Needed	Notes

Insurance

Type	Broker/Agent	Carrier	Policy Number	Where Kept

Valuables

Item	Date of Acquisition	Appraised Value/Date	Appraiser/Guide

Automobile

Vital Statistics

Make/Model/Year	Owner/Registration	Warranty	License Plate Number

Maintenance Notes

Vehicle	Inspection	Tires	Brakes	Oil, Water, Coolant, etc.	Other

Vital Documents

Wills & Guardianship

Name	Document	Attorney	Where Kept

Name	Document	Expiration Date	Where Kept

Birth Certificates

Name	Certificate Number	Where Kept

Marriage Certificates

Names	Certificate Number	Where Kept

Name	Number	Expiration Date

Name	Social Security Number
Amy Evans 321-72-1262 BD 3-12-67	
Margie Fox 216-04-4842 BD 4-13-68	
Becky Scheps 216-04-4563 BD 12-27-71	

Degrees, Awards, & Service Records

Name	Description	Date	Where Kept

Pets

Vital Statistics

Name	Breed	Date of Birth	Sex	Markings	Location of Papers

Name	Date	Vaccination	Date to Repeat

Registration

Name	License Number	Where Kept

Household Possessions

Vital Statistics

Item	Brand	Serial Number	Model Number

Item	Brand	Serial Number	Model Number

Warranties

Item	Date Purchased	Number	Issuer	Expiration Date	Where Kept

Item	Date Purchased	Number	Issuer	Expiration Date	Where Kept

Maintenance Notes

AIR CONDITIONING	
HEATING	
SECURITY	
POOL	
CHIMNEY	
GUTTERS	
FIRE EXTINGUISHER	
SMOKE DETECTOR	
OTHER	
Septic	(410) 472-2723 Groom's Septic Service 5/3/00

Family Records

Birthdays & Anniversaries

Name	Event	Date

Birthdays & Anniversaries

Name	Event	Date

Presents & Particulars

Name	Sizes	Favorite Colors	Hobbies & Interests	Wish List

Presents & Particulars

Name	Sizes	Favorite Colors	Hobbies & Interests	Wish List

A to Z Household Directory

Appliance Sales & Service

Name	Address	Phone/Fax	Notes

Architects

Name	Address	Phone/Fax	Notes

Art Dealers & Galleries

Name	Address	Phone/Fax	Notes

Athletic Facilities & Clubs

Name	Address	Phone/Fax	Notes

Automobile Clubs

Name	Address	Phone/Fax	Membership Number	Notes

Automobile Rentals

Name	Address	Phone/Fax	Notes

Automotive Service & Repair

Name	Address	Phone/Fax	Notes

A Miscellaneous

Bakeries

Name	Address	Phone/Fax	Notes

Name	Address	Phone/Fax	Notes

Beauty Services

Name	Address	Phone/Fax	Specialty	Notes

Boating Supplies & Marinas

Name	Address	Phone/Fax	Specialty	Notes

Bookstores

Name	Address	Phone/Fax	Notes

Boutiques & Small Shops

Name	Address	Phone/Fax	Notes

Butchers

Name	Address	Phone/Fax	Notes

Books for Baby Gifts

Hush, Little Baby	Sylvia Long	
The 12 Gifts of Birth	Charlene Costanzo	

Cable Television

Name	Address	Account Number	Phone/Fax	Notes

Carpenters & Cabinetmakers

Name	Address	Phone/Fax	Notes

Carpet Cleaners

Name	Address	Phone/Fax	Notes
Carpet Mill Discounters		(410) 666-0101	
Robb Lawrence			
Bridgeman Carpet Cleaners			
Al Beck		410 821-1133	

Caterers & Party Services

Name	Address	Phone/Fax	Notes

Child Care & Babysitting

Name	Address	Phone/Fax	Notes

Chimney Sweeps

Name	Address	Phone/Fax	Notes

Civic Organizations

Name	Address	Phone/Fax	Notes

Clock & Watch Repair

Name	Address	Phone/Fax	Notes

Computer Sales & Service

Name	Address	Phone/Fax	Notes

C Miscellaneous

Dentists

Name	Address	Phone/Fax	Notes

Department Stores

Name	Address	Phone/Fax	Notes

Diaper Services

Name	Address	Phone/Fax	Notes

Doctors

Name	Address	Phone/Fax	Specialty	Recommended by	Notes

Dry Cleaners

Name	Address	Phone/Fax	Notes

D Miscellaneous

Name	Address	Phone/Fax	Notes
Image Asphalt Maintenance	Pasadena, MD	1-800-760-7325	Driveway Sealer 5/99

Electricians

Name	Address	Phone/Fax	Notes

Electronics Sales & Service

Name	Address	Phone/Fax	Notes

Fabric & Notions Stores

Name	Address	Phone/Fax	Notes

Firewood Suppliers

Name	Address	Phone/Fax	Notes

Flooring & Floor Coverings

Name	Address	Phone/Fax	Notes

Florists

Name	Address	Phone/Fax	Notes

Food for Delivery & Take-Out

Name	Address	Phone/Fax	Notes

Furniture Sales, Restoration, & Repair

Name	Address	Phone/Fax	Notes

F Miscellaneous

Name	Address	Phone/Fax	Notes

Garbage Collectors

Name	Address	Phone/Fax	Notes

Garden Shops & Nurseries

Name	Address	Phone/Fax	Notes

Gourmet Shops & Delicatessens

Name	Address	Phone/Fax	Notes

Government Offices & Agencies

Name	Address	Phone/Fax	Notes

Grocery Stores

Name	Address	Phone/Fax	Notes

Hardware Stores

Name	Address	Phone/Fax	Notes
Lowe's		(410) 683-8500 M-S 6Am-10pm Sun. 8-8	

Health-care Workers & Services

Name	Address	Phone/Fax	Notes

Heating Systems

Name	Address	Phone/Fax	Notes

Hospitals & Clinics

Name	Address	Phone/Fax	Notes

Hotels & Motels

Name	Address	Phone/Fax	Notes

Housecleaning & Maid Services

Name	Address	Phone/Fax	Notes

Housesitters

Name	Address	Phone/Fax	Notes

ℋ Miscellaneous

Inns / Bed & Breakfasts

Name	Address	Phone/Fax	Notes

Insurance Agencies

Name	Address	Phone/Fax	Notes

Interior Designers

Name	Address	Phone/Fax	Notes

Investment Advisors

Name	Address	Phone/Fax	Notes

Seneca Home Inspector   Chris Snyder

Jewelry Sales & Repairs

Name	Address	Phone/Fax	Notes

7 Miscellaneous

Kennels

Name	Address	Phone/Fax	Notes

K Miscellaneous

Landscapers & Gardeners

Name	Address	Phone/Fax	Notes

Laundry Services

Name	Address	Phone/Fax	Notes

Lawn Care Services

Name	Address	Phone/Fax	Notes

Lawyers

Name	Address	Phone/Fax	Notes

Libraries

Name	Address	Phone/Fax	Notes

Lighting Supplies & Installation

Name	Address	Phone/Fax	Notes

Liquor Stores

Name	Address	Phone/Fax	Notes

Locksmiths

Name	Address	Phone/Fax	Notes

Lumberyards

Name	Address	Phone/Fax	Notes

L Miscellaneous

Mailing & Shipping Services

Name	Address	Phone/Fax	Notes

Movie Theaters

Name	Address	Phone/Fax	Notes

Moving & Storage

Name	Address	Phone/Fax	Notes

Musical Instrument Sales & Service

Name	Address	Phone/Fax	Notes

M Miscellaneous

Newspapers & News Delivery Service

Name	Address	Phone/Fax	Notes

Nursing Homes

Name	Address	Phone/Fax	Notes

N Miscellaneous

Name	Address	Phone/Fax	Notes

O Miscellaneous

Painters & Paperhangers

Name	Address	Phone/Fax	Notes
T. A. Kornick	Hurson Dulaney Valley	628	
University Painters		800-390-4848	

Pet Groomers & Trainers

Name	Address	Phone/Fax	Notes

Pet Supplies

Name	Address	Phone/Fax	Notes

Name	Address	Phone/Fax	Notes

Photographic Services (Supplies & Film Development)

Name	Address	Phone/Fax	Notes

Piano Tuners

Name	Address	Phone/Fax	Notes

Picture Framers

Name	Address	Phone/Fax	Notes

Plumbers

Name	Address	Phone/Fax	Notes

Post Offices

Name	Address	Phone/Fax	Notes

Public Transportation

Name	Address	Phone/Fax	Notes

P and Q Miscellaneous

Real Estate Agencies

Name	Address	Phone/Fax	Notes

Record Stores

Name	Address	Phone/Fax	Notes

Religion / Religious Services

Name	Address	Phone/Fax	Notes

Name	Address	Phone/Fax	Notes

Roofers

Name	Address	Phone/Fax	Notes

R Miscellaneous

Schools

Name	Address	Phone/Fax	Notes

Seafood Stores

Name	Address	Phone/Fax	Notes

Security Systems

Name	Address	Phone/Fax	Notes

Senior Citizen Centers & Organizations

Name	Address	Phone/Fax	Notes

Shoe & Handbag Repair

Name	Address	Phone/Fax	Notes

Shoe Stores

Name	Address	Phone/Fax	Notes

Snow Removal

Name	Address	Phone/Fax	Notes

Social Clubs

Name	Address	Phone/Fax	Notes

Sporting Goods Sales & Service

Name	Address	Phone/Fax	Notes

Stationers & Office Supplies

Name	Address	Phone/Fax	Notes

Swimming Pools *(Sales, Supplies, & Maintenance)*

Name	Address	Phone/Fax	Notes

S Miscellaneous

Tailors & Dressmakers

Name	Address	Phone/Fax	Notes

Taxis & Limousines

Name	Address	Phone/Fax	Notes

Textile Restoration & Repair

Name	Address	Phone/Fax	Notes

Theaters & Performance Halls

Name	Address	Phone/Fax	Notes

Ticket Agents

Name	Address	Phone/Fax	Notes

Toy Stores

Name	Address	Phone/Fax	Notes

Travel Agencies

Name	Address	Phone/Fax	Notes

Tree Surgeons & Services

Name	Address	Phone/Fax	Notes

Typing & Word Processing Services

Name	Address	Phone/Fax	Notes

T Miscellaneous

Name	Address	Phone/Fax	Notes

Utilities

<u>GAS</u>

Name	Address	Phone/Fax	Notes

<u>ELECTRICITY</u>

Name	Address	Phone/Fax	Notes

WATER

Name	Address	Phone/Fax	Notes

TELEPHONE

Name	Address	Phone/Fax	Notes

U Miscellaneous

Vegetable & Fruit Markets

Name	Address	Phone/Fax	Notes

Name	Address	Phone/Fax	Notes

Videotape Sales & Rentals

Name	Address	Phone/Fax	Notes

V Miscellaneous

Window Cleaners

Name	Address	Phone/Fax	Notes

W and X Miscellaneous

Y and Z Miscellaneous

Name	Address	Phone/Fax	Notes
Greeting Office	The White House Washington DC. 20500	6 wks advance 80th Bthy, 50th Anniversary	

More Help Not Listed

Name	Address	Phone/Fax	Notes

More Help Not Listed

Name	Address	Phone/Fax	Notes

More Help Not Listed

Name	Address	Phone/Fax	Notes

Name	Address	Phone/Fax	Notes

More Help Not Listed

Name	Address	Phone/Fax	Notes

More Help Not Listed

Name	Address	Phone/Fax	Notes

More Help Not Listed

Name	Address	Phone/Fax	Notes

Name	Address	Phone/Fax	Notes

VIKING STUDIO BOOKS
Published by the Penguin Group
Viking Penguin, a division of Penguin Books USA Inc.,
375 Hudson Street, New York, New York 10014, U.S.A.
Penguin Books Ltd, 27 Wrights Lane,
London W8 5TZ, England
Penguin Books Australia Ltd, Ringwood,
Victoria, Australia
Penguin Books Canada Ltd, 10 Alcorn Avenue, Suite 300,
Toronto, Ontario, Canada M4V 3B2
Penguin Books (N.Z.) Ltd, 182-190 Wairau Road,
Auckland 10, New Zealand

Penguin Books Ltd, Registered Offices:
Harmondsworth, Middlesex, England

First published in 1992 by Viking Penguin,
a division of Penguin Books USA Inc.

1   3   5   7   9   10   8   6   4   2

CIP data available.

Printed in Singapore
Set in Goudy Oldstyle